OH GOD!

ITS GRIMM

*The best of the Sunday funnies
from the nationally syndicated cartoon strip
Mother Goose & Grimm.*

by Mike Peters

POOCHER'S PROFILE:

GRIMM

BIRTHPLACE: A Charmin box under the kitchen sink.

HOBBY: Making macrame plant hangers out of cat hair.

LAST BOOK EATEN: *The Dogs of War*

LATEST ACCOMPLISHMENT: Catching a rabbit and then selling the hubcaps.

FAVORITE DINING SPOT: The dumpster behind McDonald's.

WHY I DO WHAT I DO: "It's a dirty job, but somebody has to do it."

QUOTE: "I'm never too busy to stop and smell the garbage."

PHILOSOPHY: I stink . . . therefore I am!

HIS FAVORITE DRINK: Toilet bowl water with a splash.

TABLE OF CONTENTS

THE THRILL OF THE CHASE

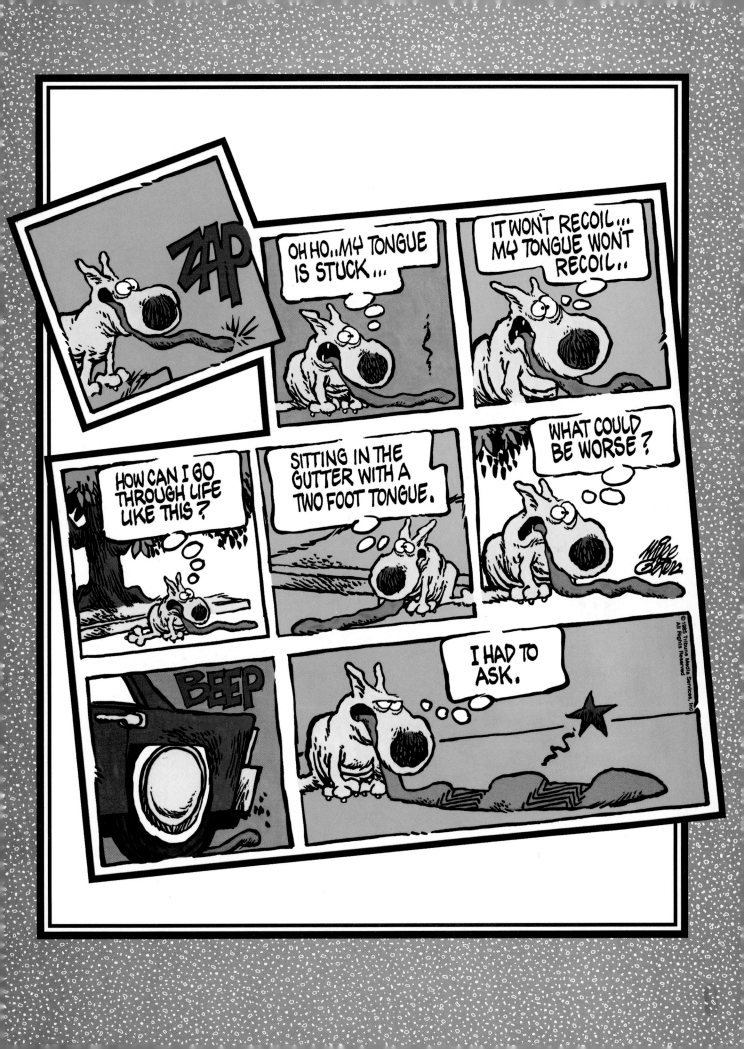

FOOD GLORIOUS FOOD

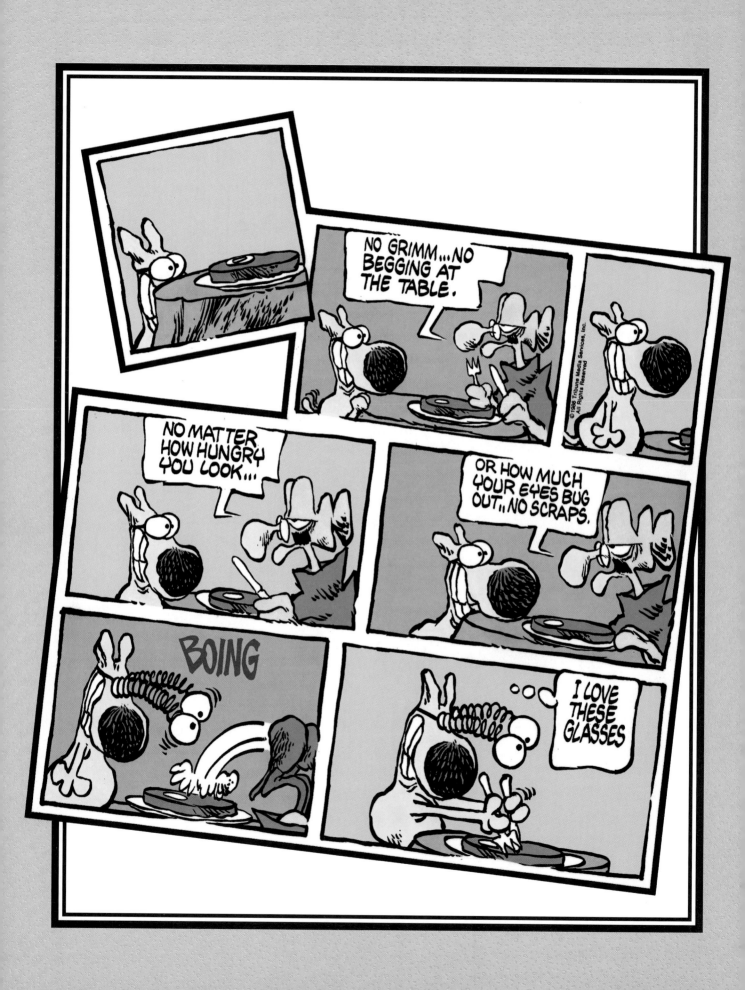

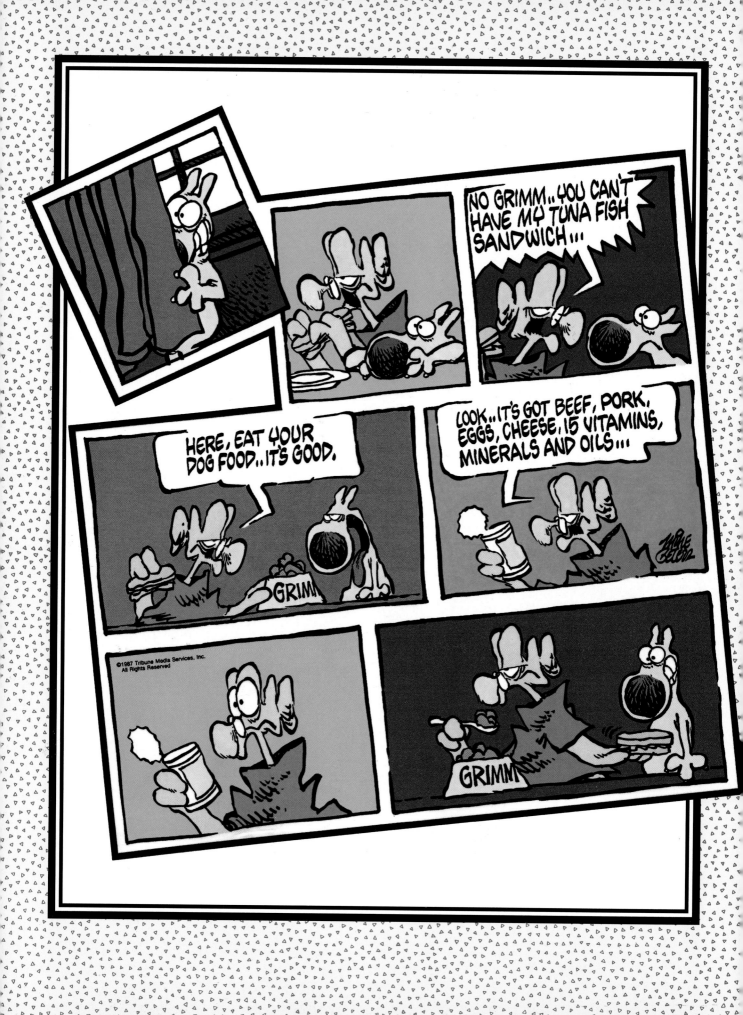